## The Library at Warwick School
Please return or renew on or before the last date below

9/14

To calypsonian Lord Kitchener
of *'London is the place for me'* fame
and to the West Indian 'Legends'

JANETTA OTTER-BARRY BOOKS

First published in Great Britain in 2010 by
Frances Lincoln Children's Books,
74-77 White Lion Street, London N1 9PF

www.franceslincoln.com

A catalogue record for this book is available from the British Library.

ISBN 978-1-84507-954-3

Set in Sabon LT

Printed and bound by CPI Group (UK) Ltd, Croydon, CR0 4YY

# Big City
## Butter-Finger

### Bob Cattell · John Agard

*Illustrated by Pam Smy*

**F**
FRANCES LINCOLN
CHILDREN'S BOOKS

# Chapter 1

Riccardo was looking down at the river swirling under Westminster Bridge as Big Ben struck the hour. The sound of the bell cut through the roar of London traffic. Bong... Bong... Bong... Nine times it struck. Nine o'clock in the evening and still daylight. The sun was shining low over the river but it was freezing cold. The people hurrying past didn't seem to notice: they were in shorts and tee shirts, dressed for a tropical summer's day in the Caribbean. Riccardo shivered.

"They got cold blood in they veins," said Count Crawfish. "Sun don't shine much in England.

When it come out it got no fire in it – it just up there in the sky like a force-ripe orange – but these English tell you it a heat-wave."

Unlike Riccardo, who was on his first visit to London, old Crawfish knew the city well. As a young man he'd starred at the Notting Hill Carnival; Riccardo had seen some old black and white photos of him, dancing through the streets with his dreadlocks flowing. That was when the Count was at the height of his calypso fame and his songs were sung all over… way beyond their little Island in the Caribbean. Nowadays his locks were

white and his professional singing days were over; he'd still perform from time to time, but only for friends and, of course, at Carnival.

Riccardo and Crawfish had met at the Island's Oval cricket ground, where the Count was the groundsman. *The day that change me life*, Riccardo called it. The old calypsonian had recognised Riccardo's songwriting talent immediately and helped him launch his singing career. And now here they were together in London. Crawfish was coming out of retirement 'for one performance only' and they were both appearing on stage at the London Caribbean Festival.

"Over there is where we singing, man," said the old poet, pointing downriver, past a gigantic wheel, at a big concrete building with a green curved roof. "That the world-famous Royal Festival Hall, Butter-Finger."

*Butter-Finger* was Riccardo's singing name. It had come from the cricket field, where his team-mates used it to tease him endlessly about his legendary clumsiness and all those catches he dropped. There wasn't much doubt that Riccardo was the worst catcher in the team. Somehow he could never get his hands together at the right moment. Wesley, the lead singer of Calypso Cricket Club's band, had even written a cruel song about Butter-Finger. But now the name had brought Riccardo calypso fame and, right across the Caribbean, Butter-Finger was a rising star.

Riccardo stared long and hard at the concert hall by the river. "It big all right!" was all he could find to say.

"Three thousand seats and every one sold out. Three thousand faces watch you sing, Butter-Finger." Count Crawfish smiled as a look of wide-eyed apprehension crept over Riccardo's face. "Eh eh, make no difference when you sing to thirty souls or three thousand... 'cept six thousand hand give louder applause."

Along the river banks, towering buildings shone pink in the evening light. Bridge after bridge spanned the swirling grey waters of the Thames. As he turned once more to look up at Big Ben and the Houses of Parliament, Riccardo Small had never felt so small in his life.

Even in his wildest imagination he'd not expected London to be so busy. It was hard to imagine the peace and tranquillity of his little Island as he stood here at the heart of this great teeming city. He thought of home: his mother and sister Martha and his dog Jessie in the kitchen of their yellow chattel house. And then his thoughts drifted to his friend Bashy and the Calypso cricket team playing in Trinidad, where they were competing, right now, in the Valentine Shield.

Riccardo would have been there with them, if it hadn't been for the Festival. He would have been playing with the team or more likely singing in the band and writing songs to spur on the players. For if there was one thing he loved even more than playing cricket, it was writing and singing songs. Playing at the Royal Festival Hall was the pinnacle of his singing career so far. It would be scary to stand in the spotlight on that big stage, but it would also be the most exciting moment of his life.

Looking up at Big Ben, Riccardo tripped on the kerb and went sprawling across the road, narrowly missing the wheels of a London taxi. Recovering his balance he found himself facing a woman standing defiantly astride a chariot, driving four wild-looking horses which for a scary moment seemed to be galloping straight towards him. "Who that girl?" he asked Count Crawfish as he realised it was just an enormous statue. "What she story?"

"That Boadicea," replied the Count. "Queen of the Iceni."

"Iceni?" asked Riccardo.

"That her tribe name. Damn fierce warrior, Boadicea. She stir up lot of trouble for Emperor Nero and his Roman Empire."

"Roman? But that ancient history, man."

"Near two thousand years ago. Boadicea – they sometime call her Boudicca today – she and she daughters up there in that chariot, they burn London to the ground. 80,000 people die in the battle. Nero and his Roman army get a proper big shake-up...."

"So what happen?"

"What you think? Romans come back with a bigger army to chase out the 'treacherous lioness' – that what they call that girl Boadicea. She take poison before they catch she. And, to this day the British say Boadicea a great freedom fighter. Shame they don't ever see the joke."

"Joke?"

"Boadicea fight for freedom against Roman Empire. But when the British get they empire, what they do? They just like the Romans. And what they call them freedom fighters who stand up against Empire? Savages, that what. When I think of Boudicca leading her army, I think of Nanny, our Jamaican heroine, leading her rebel slaves to freedom town."

Crawfish began to sing:

Boadicea
Queen of the ancient Iceni.
Boadicea
In she chariot she lead she army.
Boadicea
She was a freedom fighting lady.
Boadicea
She fight fire with fire.
Boadicea
Celtic thorn in the Roman Empire.

Now, her statue standing in the wind
Have this West Indian thinking
Of that warrior lady, Nanny.

Nanny
Queen of Jamaica blue mountains,
Nanny
To she lips she put the conch shell,
Nanny
The spark of hope when the slaves rebel,
Nanny
She fight fire with fire,
Nanny,
Ashanti thorn in the British Empire.

Count Crawfish is no scholar or history writer
But I call these two ladies freedom fighter.
Yes, in my book they were freedom fighter.

"London Town full of such stories if you care to look for them, Rikki my boy," said the Count. "So what you want see while you here? Buckingham Palace, home of the Queen Elizabeth? St Paul Cathedral? Madame Tussaud? What is top of you London story list?"

"I want see Lord's Cricket Ground," said Riccardo, without a second's hesitation. *Mecca of Cricket*, that's what Uncle Alvin always called Lord's and Riccardo had dreamed many times of making his own pilgrimage to the great ground.

"Hmm, I been thinking 'bout Lord's too," said the Count. "West Indies playing there today, you know. First test match 'gainst England. But all the tickets sold and, besides, you and me far too busy to go cricket watching all day."

Riccardo knew all about the game. He had been watching it on the television in his hotel room that very afternoon while the Count slept after the long flight. It was the first time he'd stayed in a hotel and he'd sat on his bed and flicked through all the TV channels till, to his surprise and delight, he'd come across the cricket. Things hadn't gone too well for the West Indies, however. England were 330 for three at close of play, thanks to five dropped catches.

He imagined himself in the crowd sitting in the sunshine cheering on the West Indies fast bowlers. Where was Lord's Ground, he wondered? It couldn't be too far away.

"Maybe we find time to go after the weekend," said Crawfish, reading the look of disappointment on Riccardo's face.

# Chapter 2

*Royal Festival Hall in the picture,*
*Mum… it next to the Waterloo*
*Bridge. It the place where I singing*
*on Saturday and, I tell you, it so big –*
*bigger than Constantine Bay with*
*a roof over it. Count Crawfish say*
*all the famous singers in the world*
*play here. I wish Martha and she*
*friends here to sing with me.*
*Don't let Jessie eat too much, please,*
*Mum. You know she too fat already.*
*Love from London Town.*
*Riccardo*

*Mrs I Small*
*4 Windmill Road*
*Holetown*
*The Island*
*West Indies*

Riccardo propped the postcard to his mother against the lamp on his bedside table. Alone in this strange hotel room, he was feeling homesick for the first time since his arrival. He always knew he'd miss Jessie, his dog, but things were really bad when he started missing his big sister, Martha, too.

He turned out the light. The red glow of the

city filled the little room and the noise of traffic and hum of the air conditioning rang in his ears.

There was something else that was troubling him, too. The moment he closed his eyes, he pictured his father's smiling face. His dad had come to England to look for work more than three years ago. In the early days he used to phone home and talk about London and his job in the picture-framing warehouse in a place he called Short Itch. Somehow it made Riccardo think of fleas and rats and the slums he'd read about in the books of Charles Dickens.

His mother was always happy after his dad rang and she'd tell Riccardo and Martha about her dreams of taking them both to England one day to see all the famous sights.

Then the phone calls stopped and the letters dried up too. Once Riccardo had asked his mother if she had his dad's address so he could write, and she'd snapped back, "Don't talk to me 'bout you father. He no father to you."

That had made Riccardo angry and, after that, he and his mum didn't mention his dad or London any more, though once in a while, when they were sitting together in the roti shop, Uncle Alvin would tell Riccardo funny stories about the things he and his dad got up to when they were boys.

Before he left the Island to come to London, Riccardo had intended to ask his mother if she knew where his dad lived now, but he never got round to it.

At last he fell asleep and had an unpleasant dream about the rats of Short Itch. At three in the morning the phone by his bedside rang. It was Bashy.

"Hey Riccardo, man, Bashy here. How you doing?"

"What?.... What time is it?"

"Ten o'clock. Whassup, Ricky?"

"You know what London time is?"

"No, I ringing from Trinidad, man – just call to give you the news."

Riccardo yawned.

"You know we play two games in the tournament already," Bashy persisted. His voice was loud and clear, as if he was phoning from the next room. "First one St Helena from Grenada... then today we play tournament favourites – big team from Barbados name of Coddrington College. Everyone say we don't have no chance and we back

home on the boat tomorrow. So we win the toss and bat and, man, Natty stroke a fifty."

"Did you win?" asked Riccardo sleepily.

"I comin' to that. I get 23, caught on the boundary, and Desmond 35. We 167 for eight from our overs. Ain't so big a total but it give Leo and Natty and the boys something to bowl at. But their batting strong, man. Number one and number three put down roots. Then they change the tempo – start to score quick off Leo and Rohan – and they have 100 up for just one wicket in no time."

"But did you win?" persisted Riccardo.

"I comin' to that. Natty try everything he

know … we desperate to take a wicket. And then there come this lucky run out. Their captain slip up chasing a quick single and Desmond throw down the wicket from cover point – just one stump to aim at and down it go, flat. After that man of the match, Natty, break through with two more wickets, and we back in the game."

Riccardo yawned and dropped the phone. He leaned out of bed and searched for it on the floor.

"Hello. Hello?"

"Sorry, I drop the phone," said Riccardo.

"Lucky we don't drop no catches today," said Bashy. "The fielding sharp, man. But there some bad news, too. I break my little finger and Natty's knee swollen bad. He twist it in collision with the batter."

"Did you win?"

"I comin' to that. Last over and they need six runs and Leo come back, bowling fast. First ball down the leg side. Wide. That when I break my finger, diving full stretch. Then two dot balls and a clean-bowled wicket. Three balls to go; five to win and new batter snicks a two. Then he snicks another straight into my glove. My, that hurt, man. Three to win from the last ball. It hit straight to Rohan. He fire it back to me over the stumps – ouch – but they only get one run. Game over. Calypso victors. You should have see them Coddrington College faces."

"And the first game, you win that one too? 'Gainst eh...?"

"It a knockout tournament, man! We lose and we go home."

"So who you beat?" asked Riccardo drowsily.

"St Helena. I tell you, man... you not listening. We beat them by 20 runs. Leo take five for 30. He blow them away. Leo player of the tournament so far."

"So what happen next?" said Riccardo, struggling to stay awake.

"We in the semi final on Saturday. Natty knee strapped up but he going to play. I playing too... but I can't keep wicket with broken finger." There was a short silence before Bashy added, "But hey, man? Wh'appening in London?"

"Saturday I singing at the Royal Festival Hall," said Riccardo.

"Heavy, man, better get some sleep." And Bashy rang off.

Riccardo lay thinking about the Calypso players far away in Trinidad. Natty, the captain, was a fine all-rounder and Leo was the fastest young bowler on the Island, though he could be a bit wayward at times. But Bashy, his best friend, was the true class player. Uncle Alvin said he was a West Indies wicketkeeper in the making.

Riccardo loved cricket, but playing it didn't come easy for him. Apart from the three stars in the Calypso team none of the other players were anything special – they tried hard and played together well as a team, but they weren't great cricketers. Even so, Riccardo was no better than the team's twelfth man. For a long time he'd envied

Bashy his cricketing skills, but that was before his singing had started to take off. Now he'd found something else he loved and this time he was good at it.

He began to turn around in his head a little nonsense song that had just come to him about their cricket ground on the Island. He started to hum it and then he sang out loud:

> No roller to roll,
> No mower to pass,
> When sheep turn groundsman,
> Groundsman go eat grass.
> And when bat and ball meet,
> Groundsman will bleat.

On Saturday, in the semi-final, the Calypso band would play his songs. As far as he knew, there was no other cricket club in the world with its own calypso band... the team and the musicians, led by Wesley, were inseparable.

Riccardo smiled as he imagined the boys singing about Calypso's victories in the Valentine Shield. The top young teams in the Caribbean were competing in the tournament and it was against all the odds that Calypso had won their first two games. No wonder Bashy was so excited... nobody had expected the Island team even to qualify. They said it was a miracle when they beat Windward Wanderers at home in the Island Cup. And now here they were in the semi-final.

Riccardo yawned. He started to count sheep nibbling the grass nice and short at Calypso's cricket ground. And finally he fell asleep again.

# Chapter 3

The sleek and shiny pleasure boat swept under Tower Bridge, gliding with the tide. The towers of the bridge were grey against a slate-grey sky.

The boat trip was what the organisers called a *get-to-know-you party* for all the singers and performers in the Caribbean Festival. Riccardo, leaning against the rails of the boat, hadn't got to meet a single one of them yet because a sudden squall of rain had struck just after the boat left Westminster pier, sending the passengers scurrying for the shelter of the covered seats and the bar.

Now the rain had practically stopped and Riccardo drew a crumpled envelope from the side pocket of his jacket and opened up the letter inside. It was from his father... the last letter he'd received from him, more than a year ago. He read it for the hundredth time:

*... It so-call summer now in London. Thank the Lord winter over... though the weather still cold and grey and it rain a lot but the days like they never done. This a noisy, busy place and the people don't smile too much or greet you in the street, but you get used to they ways. Food not too tasty neither – they don't care for spicy fare much in England – and it a devil of a thing to pick up a piece of saltfish anywhere. Or get pepper sauce or dasheen. But at last I find a market not too far away call Ridley Road where there plenty good West Indian ingredients to cook. So now I think of you at home while I eating my curry goat. I miss you Ricko. Maybe one day soon you come here and I show you Ridley Road and all of London Town. You be amazed, that for sure.*

His dad hadn't written him many letters and the last one was the best he'd ever sent. It had come with a picture of his father, standing in front of Nelson's column, in his best suit and with a pigeon sitting on his arm. Riccardo wondered what had happened to that photo.

And now he too found himself in London Town and, although he knew there was little chance of ever coming across his father in this teeming city, he just couldn't drive the thought out of his head. He wasn't even sure his dad still lived in London any more but that didn't stop him staring at every man of his father's build or height. He kept spotting him crossing the road or getting out of a taxi... although of course it never turned out to be his dad.

Riccardo put the letter carefully back in the envelope and stuffed it in his pocket just as Count Crawfish appeared at his shoulder.

"Ah, here you be, Rikki Tikki. You enjoying English weather?"

The Count was the only person in the world who called him *Rikki Tikki*. It was the name of a mongoose in an old story called *The Jungle Book*. Riccardo didn't mind the name too much as long as Crawfish kept it strictly for their private conversations.

"Over there the old West India docks," said the poet, pointing towards a cluster of high-rise towers. "Sugar from Jamaica, Trinidad and Barbados, bananas from Grenada. In them old days the boats from the Caribbean come in here and queue up to fill the English fruit bowls and sweeten their tea. Now the docks' days are finished and they pile them up high with banks and office buildings. They call it Canary Wharf, after Canary Islands where the ships stop off on they way home."

Riccardo looked up at the sky again. The rain had stopped.

"Ain't no wonder these Brits talk about weather all the time here," said Crawfish. "One minute you under a pressure shower and, look now, the sun almost creeping out through that cloud."

"It still so grey, though."

"Grey! Nothing wrong with grey," said the Count. "Enjoy it, is what I say." And, without drawing breath he started singing.

The British weather always get a bad press:
They say the weatherman is one man
    you can't guess,
But Count Crawfish say this grey does teach
    fair play,
Yes, this grey show democracy the way.

You can't accuse them clouds of discrimination,
They scattering their showers all 'cross
    the nation.
Each Brit getting fair share of the grey
And grey cloud for free; no,
    you don't have to pay.


Count Crawfish say enjoy the grey,
Count Crawfish say let grey make your day.
'Cos the grey unites the black and the white,
Yes, the grey unites the black and the white.

The little party of reggae and soca, calypso and
chutney singers began to emerge on to the deck,
and hearing Crawfish singing they gathered round.
Some of the biggest names in Caribbean music
were on the boat. Rasika Dindial and 'Rapsoman'
Brother Resistance had come from Trinidad.
The great Jamaican Omar 'Tarrus' Riley and
Mac Fingall from Barbados were top of the bill
on Sunday night. Count Crawfish knew them
all. He introduced them to Riccardo one by one,
reminiscing about the adventures they had shared
singing together through the years.

The second youngest member of the party,

after Riccardo, was from Martinique. She was called Christiane Cesaire and she spoke English with a sweet French twang.

Christiane was a *zouk* singer and dancer. Zouk, the music of Martinique and Guadalupe, was played on the tambour drum and the chacha, a tin can filled with stones, usually backed up by a big chorus of singers. Its strong West African rhythms made it popular in the discos.

Christiane was in London for the first time, too. She told Riccardo how nervous she was about appearing on the Festival Hall stage. "When we sing in Martinique, everybody dancing," she said. "But what I going to do with all those people sitting down looking at me?"

"What time you singing?" Riccardo asked.

"Four o'clock Sunday."

"I could come watch you, if you like," said Riccardo shyly.

"No, you dance with me on stage," said Christiane, her face brightening into a sparkling smile.

"Well... I not sure..." Riccardo's dancing wasn't much better than his fielding. He could just see himself getting his legs and arms tangled up and falling flat on his face in front of all those people.

"All performers here shall come and dance and wine with me," said Christiane. "That sure get the audience off they backsides. You a genius, Riccardo." And she gave him a big kiss on the cheek.

"Well, I don't know 'bout…"

"Riccardo, you don't let me down. Promise me."

"That building up on the hill Greenwich Observatory," said Crawfish, providing a welcome diversion. "It the home of Mean Time… where time start all over the world."

"It five hours later here than in the West Indies, did you know that?" said Christiane.

"Yes," said Riccardo. She laughed when he told her about Bashy's phone call in the middle of the night.

On deck a solitary guitarist started gently strumming… then a bongo player joined in and someone started to sing. They passed the stately white palace of the National Maritime Museum. Someone said it ought to be called the British Slave Trade Museum. Crawfish told Riccardo and Christiane that in a way this was true.

"That museum another of the great story-telling places in London," he said. "You want to know the story of all those slaves from Africa, you find it there."

"And all those famous sailors the British so proud of, they all living off the slave trade," said Christiane.

"True," said Crawfish. "Sir Francis Drake was a slave trader and Lord Nelson vote against Wilberforce in the Abolition Bill."

By the time they reached the O₂ Dome, Mac Fingall was singing *Big Belly Man*, weaving the whole length of the deck with three horns, three saxophones, a guitar and a bongo and all the other passengers strutting behind him and

singing along. The get-to-know-you party was warming up.

The boat turned round at Woolwich and headed back upriver. One by one each of the stars of the Caribbean Festival sang a song. On the banks of the River Thames people danced and cheered, revelling in the free concert provided by the little boat as it chugged slowly upstream.

As they passed back under Tower Bridge the news got around that England had been bowled out for 490 at Lord's and West Indies were struggling on 20 for three.

But Riccardo didn't hear. He was trying out a new song on this distinguished audience: a song that had just come into his head:

I'm a little pigeon
Flying out of the blue,
And I come, Lord Nelson,
To address your statue.

I go coo-coo
And give your ear a thrill,
Though I hear you voted
No to Abolition Bill.

# Chapter 4

Crawfish was right: six thousand hands clapping made a lot of noise. The applause and the cheering and whistling was for Rasika Dindial who stood at the front of the vast stage taking yet another bow. But the capacity crowd wasn't going to let 'the queen of chutney' leave without a second encore. Young and old, black, white, brown and yellow, they stood and chanted the name she was known by the world over, "Rani, Rani, Rani!"

One by one her band returned to their instruments and the whistling and stamping grew to a crescendo, until Rasika held up her hands for silence and launched straight into her encore, *Maticoor Night.*

Riccardo was waiting nervously in the wings: he was on next. He had been due on stage at eight o'clock but it was now nearly nine. It had already been a long day. After breakfast he'd had a two-hour rehearsal session with his band. They were London Trinidadians who performed calypso and soca and chutney songs all over town. There was Henderson on drums – the band's leader – Tyrone on rhythm guitar, Denesh on bass guitar and Nathaniel and Lyle on trumpet.

Riccardo was in safe hands. They were not only fine musicians, able to pick up all his songs in seconds, but they never tired of trying to improve the sound: "Trumpet too loud, drowning out the words." "Slow down the rhythm on the second verse, Henderson." "Butter-Finger, you come in late on the off beat here. Listen to me." They made it easy for him. By the end of the session Riccardo felt he'd been playing with them all his life.

"I like you songs fine, man. They come from here," said the lanky Henderson, placing his hand across his heart. Even sitting at his drums, he looked down on the little singer.

"It easy singing here with you, but…"

"You got a good fat sound, boy. Don't worry 'bout that big old stage. Henderson and the boys right behind you."

"But..."

"Listen, Riccardo. Believe me, you star of the show. Them Londoners take you to their hearts, man. And after we go to my house and we have a party like parties does be like back home. They don't celebrate too much in this country. We show them how to celebrate proper, eh?"

After the rehearsal Riccardo and Crawfish had watched the test match on TV. West Indies crashed to 195 for eight, although Chanderpaul was still there on 58.

Later they walked through the streets of south London to the stage door of the Festival Hall, where a small group of fans was waiting to catch sight of the stars. One of the older women recognised Crawfish and giggled like a young girl as she asked him for an autograph.

They were shown to a small dressing room in the basement. The Count talked incessantly as Riccardo changed into the stylish white jacket and blue jeans that his mother and Martha had helped him choose for the show. If Crawfish thought the constant chatter would help Riccardo through his stage nerves, he was wrong, and it was with a sigh of relief that the young singer finally heard the knock on the dressing room door: "Riccardo Small, on stage in five."

The audience erupted again at the end of Rasika's final encore. Riccardo gazed out from

the wings at the sea of faces that seemed to go on for ever. As the cheering died down, Henderson and the band walked out to set up their instruments. Tyrone and Denesh both gave Riccardo a friendly knuckle tap as they passed. A lively buzz of conversation filled the big auditorium, punctuated with whistles and shouts of encouragement for the new musicians as they were tuning up. It seemed Henderson and Co had plenty of fans in the audience. The two trumpets blasted out a succession of high notes, the percussion built to a crescendo and then a white-suited MC walked on and raised his hands for silence.

"First time in London."

Applause.

"First time outside his Caribbean Island."

Louder applause.

"The little star you all been waiting for... a big hand for the mighty Butter-Finger!"

Riccardo felt a gentle push from behind as Count Crawfish steered him towards the edge of the stage. And then he stepped into the spotlight that tracked him all the way to the microphone, positioned between the two guitarists. Denesh gave him a broad toothy grin. The cheers and shouts were cut short by the first chords from Tyrone's guitar and Butter-Finger launched into his act with his signature tune.

They making fun of me in calypso,
Calling me Butter-Finger and it hurt so.
They won't let me forget the catch I drop,
Teasing me till I feel like a flop.

But one day, one day I'll be a hero.
My time will come, 'King of the Willow'.
Butter-Finger will have the last laugh
When they line up for my autograph.
Yes, when I'm in the hall of cricket fame
They'll glad to know Butter-Finger name.

As the song ended, Riccardo was almost knocked off his feet. Out from the auditorium came a roar like the crash of the sea with the howl of a hurricane. He bowed to the smiling faces and then he turned to Henderson on the drums, who gave him a thumbs up and rolled straight into the next number. It was *Pigeon on Lord Nelson Statue*, the song he'd started to write on the boat.

I'm a little pigeon flying out of the blue
And I come, Lord Nelson, to address your
    statue.
I will coo-coo my point of view
Here where your one good eye can't see me,
Here where your one good arm can't catch me,
For you might be lord of naval warfare
But pigeon is boss of Trafalgar Square.

Pigeon coo-coo high, pigeon coo-coo low
Don't mind how the wind of history blow.
Pigeon coo-coo high, pigeon coo-coo low
Pigeon posing like hero for tourist photo.

Riccardo was enjoying himself now.... taking the
microphone from its stand he strutted towards
the edge of the stage, sticking his chest out like
a pigeon.

I go coo-coo and give your ear a thrill
though I hear you voted No to Abolition Bill.
I only repeating what the wind tell me
And pigeon and the wind does follow history.

There was a howl of approval from the crowd. Riccardo caught sight of Christiane standing in the wings, clapping to the rhythm and smiling. He was glad she had come to watch his act and he gave her a little wave and sang to her.

So here on your statue I perch royally,
For you might be lord of naval warfare
But pigeon is boss of Trafalgar Square.

Pigeon coo-coo high, pigeon coo-coo low,
Don't mind how the wind of history blow.
Pigeon coo-coo high, pigeon coo-coo low,
Pigeon posing like hero for tourist photo.

The audience in the front rows were out of their seats jumping and waving. As he looked down, Riccardo spotted a man who was dancing wildly and pointing up at him. In his bright orange and blue shirt he seemed to stand out from the rest of the crowd. Riccardo smiled and waved back.

Pigeon coo-coo high, pigeon coo-coo low,
Don't mind how the wind of history blow.
Pigeon coo-coo high, pigeon coo-coo low,
Pigeon posing like hero for tourist photo.

The man held his hands up to his mouth and shouted something. Riccardo stopped dead in his tracks. The photo of his father standing in Trafalgar Square flashed across his mind. The dancer opened his arms wide, jigging his head from side to side… just as his father used to do when he danced. The words of the song died in Riccardo's throat and he dropped the mike with a crash.

Immediately realising something was wrong, the band took over with an instrumental surge of trumpet and guitar. Then the drums came in and Denesh edged forward next to Riccardo, who was still staring down at his father and he, in turn, was fighting his way through the crowd towards the exit.

Denesh picked up the mike and replaced it in the stand. "Whassup, man?" he asked.

"It my father," said Riccardo weakly.

"You don't tell me your daddy coming."

"I... didn't know. I not see him for more than three year."

"What you saying, man?" said Denesh, giving Riccardo's shoulder a gentle squeeze. He unplugged his guitar and walked off stage, motioning for the drummer and trumpeters to take up the strain.

Riccardo stood motionless, staring into the void and the crowd began to sense that something unprogrammed was happening in front of them. Some pointed at Riccardo and jeered: a buzz of conversation could be heard even above the crashing cymbals and thumping drumskins.

Just as Henderson was about to collapse from exhaustion from his long solo, Denesh reappeared at Riccardo's side and took the mike. "Ladies, gentlemen, we bring you a guest star. He singing here tomorrow but he like to give you a caiso duet with his young friend, Butter-Finger. Ladies and gentlemen... Count Crawfish."

The old calypsonian walked slowly on to the stage with his arms held high to acknowledge the applause. He took the microphone from Denesh.

"So what we going to sing, maestro?" he asked Riccardo in his relaxed way, smiling at

the audience. Then he flicked off the mike and, still smiling, said quickly in Riccardo's ear, "Take the lead from me, Rikki Tikki. You got to sing... you a pro, man. Put your father out your head till later. We goin' to sing that chutney song I write for Carnival. That get them weaving and winin'."

Holding the mike between them, Crawfish sang the opening bars unaccompanied.

When I was a boy I learn this recipe
Straight from the mouth of my aunty Drupattie.
She say, listen and listen carefully
To how you make this music they call chutney.

Then the band joined in and the Count thrust the microphone in front of Riccardo. He stuttered, missed a bar and then began hesitantly:

Stir up de tempo
In de tassa...

The crowd laughed, thinking the two performers were playing some sort of musical joke. Riccardo took a deep breath...

Spice up de lingo
With masala.

Count Crawfish came in again and the two of them began to bounce the lines back and forth.

You don't have to be a Trinie
To learn this chutney recipe,
But I have to say I am very glad
I got it straight from my aunty in Trinidad.

Riccardo forgot about the crowd and his father and, staring into the eyes of his old friend, he sang louder and the crowd clapped to the rhythm and joined in the chorus.

Stir up de tempo
In de tassa,
Spice up de lingo
With masala.

Blend sweet calypso
With a curry flavour,
Boy, let it simmer
In de rhythm fire.

The song ended and the Count took his ovation. With the audience on their feet and still calling for more, he walked briskly off stage.

Quickly Henderson took them into the next number. It was another new song.... Riccardo thought it one of the best he had written. The audience thought so too.

This is the happy news channel
That don't ring no disaster bell.
This is the channel that you choose
If you like happy breaking news.

This is the happy news channel
That show the world happy and well.
But happiness they say makes dull news viewing
And TV ratings rise when war is brewing.

Even so, I, Butter-Finger reporting –
Happy breaking news I bring
Of man's humanity to man –
Today peace broke out in Afghanistan.

Here I am on the happy frontline
Standing on what used to be a landmine,
And everywhere old enemies embrace.
I can't believe I'm looking at the human race.

And news reaching us from the Middle East
That Arabs and Jews planning a feast –
Yes, they hand in hand like turtle dove,
And Palestine all peace and love.

This is the happy news channel
Wishing the world a fairy-tale ending.
So enjoy this happy news while it last.
In the distance I hear a bomb blast.

# Chapter 5

After two encores the cheering, stamping crowd finally allowed Butter-Finger to leave the stage. The applause continued and for a time it was impossible for Riccardo to hear what people were saying to him backstage. Complete strangers grinned and laughed and shook his hand. Christiane, jumping up and down, finally managed to tell him he was wonderful and she would remember the day Butter-Finger played the Royal Festival Hall for the rest of her days. Riccardo looked around for Crawfish but he was nowhere to be seen.

It was only when he left the auditorium and was sitting in the band's dressing room, listening to Dinesh and Tyrone and Lyle chatting excitedly about the gig, that Riccardo recalled his father's appearance. No one had mentioned the incident yet, but seeing a dark cloud spread over Riccardo's

face, Dinesh finally put the question that was on all their minds.

"When you say you last see your daddy?"

"Three years ago," said Riccardo. "He work in London but my mother and me not hear word of him for some time."

"Uh huh," said Dinesh.

"You sure it he?" said Lyle.

"'Course he sure," said Dinesh. "What you saying me, man, that the boy not recognise he own father?"

"It him all right," said Riccardo quietly.

"He not change much." A surge of anger ran through his body but he kept his eyes firmly on Dinesh and fought back the tears.

"Big shock like that – 'nough to send you into spin. I impress the way you keep going, Riccardo. Real impress," said Tyrone.

"Too right, man," said Dinesh.

"The stamp of a true star," said Lyle.

At that point Henderson burst into the dressing room followed by Count Crawfish.

"You not guess who this boy's father," said Henderson, pointing to Riccardo. "It Clifford Small."

"Cliffie!" said the other three, wide- eyed.

"We just see him. He say he come to see the band play. He no idea about who is this Butter-Finger feller we playing with. But when he take he seat he see this boy strutting on stage is his own born son."

"You know my father?" said Riccardo.

"'Course we do. Everybody know Cliffie. We call he Claphand Cliffie. He the best dancer in London," said Tyrone with a big grin, but the grin died with a yelp as Dinesh kicked him hard on the shin.

"We known your father a long time," said Henderson. "He always come to see us play. He so to speak a friend of the family."

"Did he say anything 'bout..." began Riccardo before the words faded away.

"He say he want to see you, Riccardo," said Crawfish quietly. "But I tell him now not the time."

"I *don't* want see him... ever," hissed Riccardo.

The Count nodded. "Time we make tracks. It been a long day."

It was only just getting dark – that eerie half dark that Riccardo had never experienced at home in the Caribbean. They made their way back to the hotel through the quiet back streets. Crawfish remained silent for some time, but then he said, "I know you got a lot on the chest. But now the time to get it off, if you want."

Riccardo looked away.

"They call him Claphand Cliffie," said Crawfish, "because when he arrive in London he have big trouble pronouncing place names. Like he say Short Itch for Shoreditch and Tottingham and Pickled-lily. They give him Claphand name 'cos that what he say for Clapham Common and because he always clap when he dance."

"I not interested."

"I think you best had see the truth though," said the Count. "I know your dad vex with himself because he love you and Martha and he know he hurt you."

"Hurt me? He forget all about us." Riccardo's eyes blazed with anger again.

"Not forget. I know what you father like. He not proud 'bout what he done. Yes you can call it weakness... for weakness it is."

"I don't care. He don't mean nothing to me."

"Still, you remember, it take strength to come to a strange city to earn money for he family. He live a lonely life but he work hard and he make friends. And in the end he meet this girl and ..."

"He shack up with a woman?" Riccardo spat out the question.

"Yes. He have a friend."

"Who is she? Who this..." Riccardo stammered.

"You want to know any more you have to ask your father."

"I tell you, I never want see him again."

"That your decision, Riccardo. And I ain't saying no more 'bout it. Best you sleep on it, Maybe you think different in the morning."

The postcard that Riccardo wrote home that evening made no mention of his father.

---

*Ma, I missing you too much here in this city. Tonight I sing at Royal Festival Hall and you should hear the crowd cheer. They call me back for two encores and the stamping and the whistling still ring in my ear. But now I back at the hotel and I only wish I back home with you. It two days 'fore I fly back to Trinidad and I can't wait for them to pass and I back home with you.*
*Love to Martha and to Jessie.*
*Your loving son, Riccardo*

*Mrs I Small*
*4 Windmill Road*
*Holetown*
*The Island*
*West Indies*

---

As he wrote, the face in the crowd kept appearing before him. This was the man who had taught him how to catch flying fish and cook them on the beach with brushwood; who'd helped him to read and bought books for him; who'd taught him to swim and dive and play cricket and basketball. He'd even encouraged him to sing in the days before he met Count Crawfish. And then he'd betrayed him.

# Chapter 6

Ridley Road market was a little island of Caribbean life smack in the middle of north London. When they arrived the sun came out, as if to welcome Riccardo and Crawfish to the busy stalls selling their familiar West Indian wares: custard apples, bread fruit, mangos, pumpkins, sweet potatoes, puna yams, smoked fish heads, even cows' feet.

When Crawfish had said they were going to Ridley Road, Riccardo hadn't really listened. To be honest they'd hardly spoken to each other all morning. Riccardo sat in front of the television watching the test match. It had done nothing to improve his mood. West Indies had been forced to follow on and they had already lost one wicket in their second innings.

It was only when they arrived at the market that Riccardo recalled it was the very place his father had written about in his letter. His dad had come here for the tasty West Indian food he missed so much in London.

The traders kept up a constant patter: "Here we go. Fifty pence for yer lemons. Cheapest you find in London, girl. Whay you wait for... you thiefing me at that price." Reggae blasted out of portable stereos. People pushed their way through the throng, but they looked you in the eye and smiled as they squeezed past.

The crowd seemed to have gathered from everywhere on Earth: Jamaicans, Trinidadians, Bajans, Chinese, Turkish, Indians, Africans – all looking for their bargain-priced trainers, hot chillies, health remedies and pots and pans – speaking in their own languages, which melted together into the general hubbub. It was scruffy and noisy but alive like nowhere Riccardo had seen in London till now.

He passed a fishmonger with a radio held close to his ear. "West Indies heading for defeat at Lord's," said the man, smiling as he delivered the bad news. "65 for three in second innings. They need 160 more to make England bat again."

"Chanderpaul still there?" asked Riccardo.

"Yes, man. He make England work for they victory. But only hope, rain stop play."

Crawfish was busy loading mountains of food into a huge straw basket he'd just bought. There was saltfish, sweet pepper, chillies, limes, ackee, pig's feet, mangoes, roti bread, and sweet potatoes – everything purchased through fierce but jovial haggling with the stallholders. He even made up a poem for the old man on the fruit and veg stall.

No bad feelings come between fruit and veg,
Apple and Mango converse cosily,
Ripe Plantain have no quarrel with Broccoli.
Yes, my friends, in this market it's clear to see
Apple and Mango does get on socially,
The red, yellow and green live in harmony.

There was a hullabaloo of laughter round the stall, which rose to a crescendo when the old stall-holder knocked a pound off Crawfish's bill in appreciation of the poem.

"All this food! What we buy it for?" asked Riccardo, taking a hold of the heavy basket.

"We having a party," said Crawfish. "I promise the band that after I sing, I cook them the best Caribbean feast they ever taste in they lives." He inspected the food in his basket and then glanced at his watch. "Speaking of singing, we should be getting back. I on stage in one hour flat."

"One hour!" Riccardo was aghast. "What you do about getting changed and having a sound check? Come on, hurry, man."

"Take it easy, Rikki Tik," said Crawfish. "Relax, man. We plenty of time. We get a taxi."

Riccardo, who liked to sit completely alone for at least an hour to get his mind fresh before he went on stage, shook his head in disbelief.

"We all different," said the Count with a chuckle. "Sit back stage too long and, man, you start getting nervous."

In the end Riccardo had no cause to worry. It was nearly two hours before Count Crawfish finally walked out in front of the Festival Hall audience – all the acts were over-running again.

From the moment he waved at the crowd from the back of the stage, the Count's performance was a revelation. Riccardo knew, of course, that his old friend could work an audience – he'd seen him do that plenty of times before, especially at Carnival. But this concert was different. The Count, in his own words, was "coming out of retirement", and there wouldn't be many in the audience who remembered him in his glory days.

As Crawfish sauntered out into the spotlight the years seemed to slip away. The crowd was spellbound after the first few chords of his opening number. It was a song Riccardo had never heard before... called *Fresh Water Cockney*, a tale about London West Indians. The audience loved it. The Count followed up with his own version of the famous Lord Shorty song, *Watch Out My Children* and then went straight into a very rude soca-style composition entitled *Maracas Bay*.

Only then did the old calypsonian sing some of the songs that had made his name, like

*That ain't cricket, man* and *Jouvay Jumbie*.
The crowd clapped and whistled as Crawfish
danced into the auditorium with *Las' Lap Wining* –
a song about an old man who couldn't stop dancing.
Soon everyone was on their feet. The pan bands
joined in and London's Royal Festival Hall began
to look just like a Carnival street back home.

The sweat was pouring off Crawfish's brow
at the end of the number. He bowed to the
audience and attempted to leave the stage, but they
stamped their feet and whistled and called him
back. So he gave them one final song.

Riccardo recognised the little poem the
Count had made up for the Ridley Road fruit and
veg man – but now the poem had become a fully
fledged calypso, even though Crawfish hadn't
written down a word... the words and the music of
the new song were all in his head.

To get a taste of this thing diversity
I went to a market in London's fair city.
I met up Ackee and thought Saltfish must be near,
'Cos Ackee and Saltfish make a fine pair.
Then I saw Saltfish having a chat with Sausage,
You'd swear these two talking the same language.

Look how fish and meat show each other respect,
I never see a fight between two fillet yet.
And no bad feelings come between fruit and veg,
Apple and Mango converse cosily,
Ripe Plantain have no quarrel with Broccoli.
Yes, my friends, in this market it's clear to see
Apple and Mango does get on socially,
The red, yellow and green live in harmony.

I remember once right there in Brick Lane
I shook hands with my old friend Sugar Cane.
We chatted a while 'bout bittersweet history,
Then Sugar Cane introduce me to Strawberry.
Strawberry said she was just back
    from Wimbledon
And was meeting Papaw somewhere in Brixton.
I said give my regards to the old fellow,
I knew Papaw long before he turned yellow.

Look how fish and meat show each other respect,
I never see a fight between two fillet yet.
And no bad feelings come between fruit and veg,
Apple and Mango converse cosily,
Ripe Plantain have no quarrel with Broccoli.
Yes, my friends, in this market it's clear to see

Apple and Mango does get on socially,
The red, yellow and green live in harmony.

Just then a voice say, 'Crawfish, man, how you
do?'
It was Banana calling me name out of the blue.
I say, how you like this diversity thing?
Banana say, Crawfish, where do I begin?
When I feel the bite of wintry weather
I only wish I was born Chilli Pepper.
I know I'd miss how my skin slip and slide,
But Chilli will have central heating inside.


And when he finished they made him sing it all over
again.

Christiane followed Crawfish onto the stage.
She didn't have to worry about the crowd staying
in their seats. The Count had warmed them up
so much that they were rocking in the aisles even
before she broke into song. Christiane's brand of
disco zouk was just what they were waiting for.

To Riccardo's amazement, quiet Christiane hit
the stage like a wild animal... *toom-cheek, toom-cheek*... she drove on the percussion and the beat

grew louder and louder. The tempo never let up for one minute; Christiane wriggled and wined, driven on by the whistles of the crowd. She soon dragged on stage all those watching from the wings, including Crawfish and Riccardo.

The dancing got faster and faster and the crowd was driven to new heights of excitement. The songs were all in the French creole of Martinique but, after three up-tempo dance songs, Christiane announced with a big smile that she was going to sing a song in English.

"I write this specially for my new friend, Butter-Finger," she said. "We don't play cricket on Martinique. Instead we have croissants and boule and good cooking. But Riccardo, he love cricket so much: so my song just for him."

She took Riccardo's hand and the audience laughed as he shuffled nervously to the front of the stage. What was Christiane going to sing? He soon found out.

Bat and Ball were always arguing –
Bat boasting he strokes, Ball boasting she swing,
So umpires make a decision
Let Bat and Ball have a dance competition.

When de drum roll, Ball decide to keep low
And show off she version of limbo,
Yes, Ball keeping low and the crowd want more
But Bat feeling too shy to take the floor.

Christiane bowled an imaginary cricket ball at Riccardo and then began to limbo. Someone in the crowd shouted, "Play down the line, Butter-Finger." And there was more laughter.

Bat say I sure my spine go crack,
Already I feel a twinge in me back.
No, this limbo thing is not for me,
Lying low don't come naturally.
Meanwhile the crowd forming a ring

And Ball strutting she bounce and she swing.
If you see Ball moving through the air
Dancing she salsa with a latin flair.

Now Ball behaving like a disco queen
And Bat wishing he was back on the green –
I'd gladly do the hook or the cover-drive
But you won't catch me doing the jive.

Christiane pushed Riccardo to the edge of the stage,
encouraging the crowd to sing along:

The crowd shouting, Bat, show us yuh moves,
The crowd shouting, Bat, get in the groove.
So Bat give a twirl to show what he could do,
He doing the split but he ain't splitting in two.

Ball say, Bat you my friend though I might laugh
And I don't want you for split in two half.
Do the split again but don't split in two,
I don't want this split to embarrass you.

Riccardo tried his best to do the splits, egged on
by the crowd, but he toppled over and rolled on
his back. The laughter turned into a chant of

encouragement as Count Crawfish again came to
Riccardo's rescue. He shimmied to the front of
the stage and there was a huge cheer as he turned
towards Christiane and did the splits and bounced
straight back on to his feet again in one motion.
And she sang:

Do the split again but don't split in two,
I don't want this split to embarrass you.

And Crawfish sang:

I'd gladly play the wrist or the finger spin
But you won't catch me do the split again.

The dancing on stage grew wilder as more and more of the performers joined in the party. In the auditorium there was pandemonium: everyone was on their feet, stomping and clapping to the tambour rhythm. The huge crowd surged back and forth like a mighty ocean and Christiane danced on. After an hour, she had danced them all off their feet.

"This girl trow real good wais'," gasped Crawfish, dragging himself off stage, gasping for breath. "I finish, man. I hang up me singing and dancing boots for good this time."

# Chapter 7

Later that evening Riccardo, Crawfish and Christiane boarded the number 35 bus to Shoreditch with their big bags of food. The afternoon's concert was still fresh in their minds and there was so much talking and laughing that they missed their stop and the short walk to Henderson's home became a much longer one through the streets of the East End. As they made their way along, asking directions from time to time, Riccardo kept an eye out for the picture frame warehouse where his father worked... if this was Shoreditch it couldn't be far away.

Henderson lived on the sixth floor of a block of flats and from the window you could see right across London towards the river. He pointed out Tower Bridge and the Tower of London to Riccardo and Christiane. The skyscrapers of Canary Wharf loomed in the distance.

Count Crawfish made a beeline for the kitchen and started cooking. There were maybe 20 people in the big flat when they arrived, including Tyrone and Lyle. Nathaniel arrived soon after and then Dinesh with his family and within half an hour the number of guests had more than doubled and the dancing had started. There were big women dancing with thin men and old men dancing with pretty young women, and children dancing together in groups of three or four. Riccardo had a dance with Christiane, and nearly knocked over a table at which two elderly fellows with white hair and flowing white beards were playing a noisy game of dominoes.

Before long the music went live. Tyrone and Denesh took up their guitars, Henderson joined them on bongo and Denesh's wife, who had a deep folksy voice, sang:

I do not love thee
So I'll not deceive thee…

A tall woman came and stood next to Riccardo. She reminded him in a way of his mother, only she was younger and considerably thinner.

I do not love thee
Yet I'm loath to leave thee...

"Are you Riccardo Small?" the woman asked politely.

"Yes," said Riccardo.

"Hi, I'm Naomi, though everybody here call me Nanny."

"Like the mountain queen?" said Riccardo.

"Yes. I get my name from that girl. What you know about her?"

"She was freedom fighter. She stood up against the British in Jamaica," said Riccardo authoritatively.

"It's true," said the woman, smiling. "Nanny was a great woman, the leader of the Jamaican Maroons, the runaway slaves. She inspired the rebellions that forced the British Government to abolish slavery."

"You from Jamaica, too?"

"My mother was – she first to call me *Nanny*. I was

born here... in Brixton – that south of the river."
Nanny pointed towards the Thames, smiling
nervously, and then she said almost in a whisper,
"You know your father here?"

Riccardo's eyes scoured the room in panic.

I do not love thee,
Yet when gone I sigh
And think about thee
Till the stars all die...

"He in the kitchen with Crawfish. He want
to talk to you," said Nanny.

"And you ...."

"I came with him. He tell me you a great
singer."

So, thought Riccardo, this is the woman.
He'd not expected her to be like this. He didn't
want her to be pretty and have kind eyes.

"You may not care to receive advice from
me," said Nanny. "But I going to tell you anyway.
I think you regret it if you refuse to see your
father."

"And what you know about it?" blurted out
Riccardo rudely.

"I know he talks about you and your sister Martha all the time."

Riccardo stared at the kitchen door. The music stopped and was replaced by a brief moment of silence.

"Go and see him," said Nanny. "After that we'll leave, I promise."

Riccardo walked across the room, feeling that every eye was on him, and opened the door into the kitchen. Crawfish and his father were chopping vegetables together, laughing and joking. They saw Riccardo and fell silent.

"I leave you two alone," said the Count, getting up.

"No, stay, man," said Riccardo's father. "I want you to hear what I going to say. Sit down here, Riccardo."

Without a word Riccardo joined his father at the kitchen table and Clifford Small began to speak. He told Riccardo about his first year in London and finding his job with the picture frame makers and eventually becoming a foreman. He'd met Nanny and her friends that first winter and through them he'd got to know Henderson and the band and some of the artists that worked in 'Short Itch'. Suddenly London was not such a lonely place and the Island was a long way away.

"So you forget about us," said Riccardo under his breath.

"No, never. But I have plenty on my mind. I work long hours at the warehouse. And I have my new house in Claphand to knock to shape... and then the baby come along."

"Baby!"

"Nanny and me, we have a little girl. She ten months now and she beautiful. She name Keandra."

Crawfish placed his large hand on top of Riccardo's and tilted his head in his familiar way.

"It time Keandra meet she brother," said Riccardo's father. "You come say hello 'fore you go back?"

"Forget it," said Riccardo, pulling his hand away. He wanted to say a lot more but the right words wouldn't come out.

"You mind me of when I was a boy," said his dad. "My ma cut me tail if I play in the street and when I get lash I go 'way vexed. And I know how you feel, son, because my daddy he run away, too."

"Wha' scene you on?" said Riccardo. His voice was shrill but he wasn't shouting. "My ma don't give me no lash and I never do what my daddy did. And I never leave my family for some London fancy girl."

"Thank you for listening, son," said his father, getting up. "Time we go. Nanny got to work early tomorrow. It the last day of the test match."

"Test match?" said Riccardo, in spite of himself.

"Yes, She work at Lord's cricket ground. She MCC press officer."

"Then she can get us tickets for the game?" said Crawfish, looking at Riccardo with a glint of mischief in his eyes.

"No problem. But I don't know how much cricket you see. West Indies down to last three batters. I say it all over in an hour tomorrow morning. Maybe less."

Clifford Small took a step towards Riccardo as if he wanted to give him a hug, but then he thought better of it and strode out of the kitchen.

After the door closed, Riccardo and Count Crawfish sat in silence for a while. Then the Count spoke up.

"I never been married and I don't know much 'bout what they call 'parenting'," he said. "But I know that you mummy and you daddy both proud of you. And they both fine people. Maybe there only one secret of good parenting: let you children make their own mistakes but be around when they want shoulder to cry on."

He tapped a kitchen knife on the chopping board and sang quietly in his deep lilting voice:

Little monkey jump on a branch,
Lord, the branch break.
Mother monkey she say
Children must make their own mistake.

Little fish nibble the bait,
Thank God the fish escape.
Mother fish she say
Children must make their own mistake.

Little puppy playing with twig,
Twig turn out to be a snake.
Mother dog she say
Run, my puppy, run, before it too late.

Riccardo sat sullenly through the performance. When it came to an end, Crawfish gave him a crafty look and said, "So shall we go to Lord's tomorrow, Rikki Tikki? What you say to that?"

# Chapter 8

"Game over for West Indies before lunch," said a Trinidadian, standing by the W G Grace gate. He was offering the same gloomy prediction to anyone entering the ground who cared to listen.

Riccardo and Count Crawfish squeezed through the turnstyle. People with enormous picnic hampers scurried past; old men in red and yellow striped jackets and ties stood in groups talking loudly; a jazz band was playing a New Orleans stomp. After the hustle of the London streets it was like entering an ancient lost world.

Play on the final day was due to start in an hour, at 11 o'clock, though no one expected to see much cricket. West Indies were in deep trouble. They had batted better in their second innings but they still needed 95 to make England bat again, with only two wickets left.

"Two balls enough to finish the game," said Crawfish.

Riccardo didn't care. Here he was at last at the *Mecca of Cricket* and he felt like a small boy in a toy shop. He caught a glimpse of the ground between two stands. It was the greenest green he'd ever seen. In the centre the covers were being removed from the wicket and a mower was going up and down, creating beautifully straight broad stripes between the sightscreens. And there, in front of him, were all the West Indian and English players doing their warm-up exercises. Riccardo stared at the scene in disbelief.

He'd wanted to tell Crawfish that he would never ever accept the tickets, which had arrived at their hotel that morning. But the attraction of Lord's had been too strong and he soon put his scruples aside. Standing there looking at the ground for the first time, he was so happy that he found himself singing the little song that had been running through his head all morning.

I ain't in no rush
To see Trafalgar Square,
I know Lord Nelson bound to be there,

He and he pigeon ain't going nowhere.
To Trafalgar Square I have to say no,
Lord's is the place I want to go.

I ain't making tracks
To Madame Tussaud. I don't care
How many tourists that museum attracts.
I don't want to see people smiling in wax.
To Madame Tussaud's I have to say no,
Lord's is the place I want to go.

Buckingham might have a famous gate
With guards saluting the royal state,
But I mean to salute the cricket greats.
To Buckingham Palace I have to say no,
Lord's is the place I want to go.

Crawfish, Crawfish, take me to Lord's,
I want to see all dem cricket records;
Yes, Lord's is de only place for me,
I want soak up bat and ball history.

"You song make me homesick," said a voice at his shoulder. He turned to see Crawfish embracing a smartly dressed man in a black blazer.

"Brian Lara!" gasped Riccardo.

"Hey, Crawfish man, I hear you singing in London," said Lara. "You with this young calypsonian?"

"This Riccardo Small from our Island, only he better known as the mighty Butter-Finger," said the Count, pushing Riccardo forward to shake hands with the great cricketer.

"You... you know each other?" stammered Riccardo.

"Friends twenty years," said Lara with a laugh. "I Count Crawfish biggest fan."

Brian Lara told them that he had just flown in from Trinidad to open a new exhibition at the Lord's Museum – *West Indies Legends*, it was called. The opening ceremony was in half an hour and he insisted that Crawfish and Riccardo came along as his personal guests.

"Chance for young Riccardo to hear 'bout them days when West Indies cricket team rule the world," he said.

"First we take a turn of the ground," said Crawfish.

Riccardo was in a daze as they walked slowly round Lord's. He knew all Lara's cricket records:

batting average in tests, 52.88, and that record score of 400 not out in Antigua against England. The Count told him that he and Lara had first met at a concert in Trinidad, when the young batter had just become Trinidad and Tobago's youngest captain and had led them to victory over all the other islands.

"I there too when he riding Gillespie and McGrath into the breeze and single-handed he defeat Australia," said Crawfish, adding that there were only three batters he had seen who possessed true genius: Sir Garry Sobers, Sir Viv Richards and the great Brian Lara.

They stopped and watched the English bowlers bowling like the wind in the nets at the Nursery End. Then they headed for the Lord's Museum.

The first person Riccardo saw when they entered the red-brick building was Nanny. She was talking to Brian Lara and some of the other Legends. Riccardo recognised Garry Sobers, Viv Richards, Courtney Walsh, Michael Holding... and wasn't that tall one with glasses the great Clive Lloyd? Nanny waved at Riccardo and Crawfish. Riccardo stared back at her, overcome by a bewildering flood of emotions... seeing her here surrounded by his heroes.

Who had told him about the great victories of Clive Lloyd's team over Australia and England? Who had described 'Whispering Death' running up to bowl? And Richards' great innings of 291 at the Oval? And Garry Sobers six sixes in an over? Who else but his father. And here they all were, these Legends, talking cheerfully to the woman who had taken his father away from him.

When the speeches started upstairs in the exhibition area, Riccardo wandered down to a quiet corner of the museum. In a display cabinet he noticed a cricket ball, stained brown with age. A label explained that it had been the ball thrown by Joe Solomon in the first ever tied test at Brisbane in 1960. Riccardo's dad had told him the story many times: Australia were cruising to victory, but two wickets fell in the last over. Then with the scores level, Joe scored a direct hit on the stumps and ran out Ian Meckiff. Australia all out... and West Indies had tied the test.

Below the ball in the display cabinet was an old cricket bat. It had belonged to Denis Compton of England. With it he'd scored 3,816 runs in one season including 18 centuries. They must have

made bats better in those days, thought Riccardo.
He pulled his little red song book out of his pocket
and began to write:

Solitary cricket bat leaning
In a corner of a museum.
For you, no standing ovation.

Runs and willow days fill all your dreaming.
Fixed glass – your short yet O so far boundary.

Solitary cricket ball caught between
The safe fingers of posterity.
Where is your spin? Where is your reverse
   swing?
Time has stolen your fire and your sheen.
And, at this stage, it's no use appealing.

All the glass cabinets and exhibits told the history of cricket in their own peculiar way. Over there were the Ashes in their little urn. And, close by, a portrait of W G Grace. Strangest of all was another cricket ball with a dead sparrow mounted on top of it. The label said that the bird had been hit in mid flight by the ball, delivered by Jehangir Khan in the MCC v Cambridge University fixture of 1936.

A ripple of applause and the buzz of conversation brought Riccardo back to the present. The speeches had finished and he made his way cautiously up the stairs to rejoin the party. There was no sign of Nanny, so he edged forward and spotted Crawfish talking to Brian Lara. They were standing in front of a striking painting of Lara, portraying him in a pair of white shorts, chest bared.

"Brian telling me 'bout Valentine Shield," said Count Crawfish.

"And a team called Calypso Cricket Club," said Lara with a chuckle.

Riccardo blinked in disbelief. "You know Calypso...."

"They got some keen young players... remind me when I play cricket for my school and after I'd climb up the slope to pick mangoes and cashews 'fore my daddy arrive to take me home."

"You see them play!"

"Only yesterday," said Lara. "I sponsor the game. And then your team spoil my day and beat Trinidad cricket team."

"They won? Man!" Both Lara and Crawfish laughed as Riccardo punched the air.

"They win by three wickets," said Lara. "They play Alligator Pond, team from Jamaica, in the final."

"When?"

"Tomorrow."

"Who scored the runs? Did you see Bashy... I mean the keeper? Did he bat well?"

"Whoa," said Lara. "I tell you all about the

game later. Now it's time to watch some test match cricket."

"Brian invite us to join him in his hospitality box," said Crawfish.

"Chance for you to meet some West Indies Legends face to face," said Lara, smiling.

# Chapter 9

When they left the museum everyone was surprised to find that it was raining heavily. Brian Lara's box was in the Tavern stand and one by one the West Indies Legends drifted in and stood under large umbrellas, watching the rain pouring off the pitch covers.

"Soon clear up," said Michael Holding cheerfully.

"Not sure we want it clear up," said Lara, looking up at the sky.

"Rain stop play not the West Indies way to save a game," said Sir Viv.

Michael Holding asked Riccardo about the Festival Hall gig. *Whispering Death,* as Uncle Alvin used to call him, was probably the greatest fast bowler who ever lived, though it was hard to imagine this gentle person inspiring fear in the hearts of the finest batters the world over. What would Alvin say, wondered Riccardo, if he could see them now, talking together about ska and reggae? Mind you, it was Holding's thoughts on cricket not music that Riccardo really wanted to hear and finally he overcame his embarrassment and blurted out a direct question.

"What was your best day at a test match?"

"Day we beat Australia for first time on their own soil," said Holding. "Close second comes that game at the Oval here in London."

"What happen?"

"I took 14 wickets against England. Nine of them were clean bowled. I don't believe I ever bowled faster than that game. Two fifers plus!" A glimmer of menace came into the great bowler's eyes and Riccardo began to get a feeling of what facing *Whispering Death* on a fast track might be like.

The rain finally stopped. The umpires came out to look at the pitch and an early lunch was announced. Play would start at one o'clock if no more rain fell. Lunch for the Legends was curry goat and rice. Riccardo was too excited to eat, though it smelt good and he noticed that Courtney Walsh and Sir Viv had two big platefuls each.

At five to one a bell sounded and moments later the umpires walked out under brooding skies. Play was going to begin at last.

The crowd cheered out the England team, who bounced down the steps of the pavilion and went into a huddle, with Sir Viv and Sir Garry looking on with a wry smirk. There was polite applause from the crowd for Chanderpaul and Powell when they appeared.

West Indies' only realistic chance of snatching a draw lay with the weather and with Chanderpaul. The English bowlers had not yet devised a successful plan for taking his wicket in the entire match. In the first innings he had made 75 not out, and now he was unbeaten on 92. The big question seemed to be: would he get his century or run out of partners?

Michael Holding, Sir Viv and the other Legends took their seats and, looking out for Count Crawfish, Riccardo found his mentor deep in conversation with Brian Lara.

"We just talking about you," said the old poet to Riccardo. "You don't mind if you father and Nanny join us?"

The suddenness of the question took Riccardo by surprise. He shot a glance at Lara and said, "Don't mind. It up to you."

"Then I say we go and watch the cricket," said Lara, putting an arm round Riccardo's shoulder.

The England bowlers made the most of the swinging, overcast conditions but, though the ball went past Powell's bat plenty of times, they couldn't achieve the breakthrough. Chanderpaul's score crept up run by run. He was on 98 when Clifford Small sat down in the empty seat next to his son.

"Chanderpaul handling the bouncers like water on the duck back," said his father.

Riccardo nodded but stared ahead and said nothing. He noticed Nanny standing talking to Sir Viv and, watching them, missed the moment that disaster struck. After batting sensibly for half an hour Powell had a sudden rush of blood to the head. He swung wildly at a ball outside the off stump and it looped gently in the air to mid-off who took the catch. There were groans all round the box and triumphant cheers from the crowd. .

"No shot to play when you partner on 98," said Riccardo's father, shaking his head.

Riccardo said nothing. He half blamed his father and Nanny for the fall of the wicket.

The new batter was Jerome Taylor. The Legends all agreed that Taylor was a born number 11 and he wouldn't hold up the England bowlers for too long. But he scored a single off his first ball and Chanderpaul faced the last delivery of the over. A hush came over the ground as the crowd anticipated his century.

The bowler ran in and bowled. Chanderpaul stepped out to a wideish ball and drove it handsomely for four. Everyone leapt to their feet. Chanderpaul's ton had been another gritty rather than beautiful performance but even the great West Indies Legends recognised his courage and batting skill.

"Take real guts to play innings like that," said Riccardo's father, still applauding the century when everyone else had stopped.

Riccardo said nothing.

The umpires came together again, holding up their light metres. But they decided play could go on, even though it had become very dark and the lights on the scoreboard were shining out like beacons in the gloom. Taylor played and missed twice and then survived a huge shout for lbw.

"Matter of time," sighed Brian Lara.

"I amaze at how those fellers think you can bat in this light," said Riccardo's dad. As soon as he spoke there was a break in the clouds and the sun came out again.

Riccardo said nothing.

His father groaned, "Nothing going to stop them now."

Taylor missed again and the bowler put his hands up to his head in frustration and shouted something at the batter. He ran in again cheered on by the crowd. Then as he approached the bowling crease, he stopped dead in his tracks. There was a ripple of laughter from the crowd on the far side of the ground. Everyone in the box strained forward to see what was going on.

"A pigeon," said Lara.

"It land on the pitch just when the bowler running in," said Sir Viv.

The laughter grew louder as the England players tried to shoo the bird away and it hovered above their heads, only to settle again on a length as the bowler tried to bowl.

The umpires scratched their heads and tried their best to drive the pigeon off. They waved their arms. They ran at it. They called on the ground staff to try and catch it. They even brought on a man with a net. But it was all to no avail. Every time it looked as if the pigeon had departed and the bowler ran up to bowl the bird would flutter down onto the pitch again and stop the proceedings.

Five minutes passed and then ten. The crowd was getting restless. Riccardo glanced up at the sky, which was growing darker by the minute.

"That pigeon supporting West Indies," said Crawfish.

"Funny thing, you don't see too many pigeons at Lord's," said Sir Viv. "Plenty at the Oval, but not here."

"Maybe he fly in from Trinidad," said Lara.

Now the bird had taken to hovering above the England players' heads, fluttering out of reach as they jumped up and tried to snatch at its feet.

The sky grew darker and darker. A few umbrellas went up in the crowd. Then the heavens opened and it rained like it rains in the Caribbean.

The players all ran from the field and the pigeon strutted behind them towards the pavilion as if he was rounding them up like a sheep dog. Finally he took off and flew round the ground on a lap of honour.

The Legends laughed and cheered as the bird did its fly past and when the cheering died down, Riccardo turned and faced them and sang this song in the rain:

I heard of rain stopping play,
I heard of bad light causing delay,
But I live to see the day
When England was leading
And a pigeon stop the proceedings.

O Lord, it raining at Lord's,
And this time don't blame the English weather,
Blame that little fellow puffing out he feather.

Yes, England was cruising to victory
But just when West Indies think all was lost
A pigeon decide to show who was the boss.
Yes, the pigeon descend out of the blue,
Like an angel come to West Indies rescue.

England captain busy shaking he cap
But that pigeon wing in no mood to flap.
Yes, that pigeon refuse to budge from
     the crease,
A God-sent saviour for the West Indies.

Wonders never cease but daily increase,
For while the pigeon was taking centre stage
Lords turning grey and storm starting to rage.
So West Indies save defeat when lightning flash
But I say make pigeon the man of the match.

O Lord, it raining at Lord's,
And this time don't blame the English weather,
Blame that little fellow puffing out he feather.


Clifford Small took his son in his arms. "I not know which one to hug, son... you or the pigeon," he said. "But you here and the pigeon not."

Riccardo laughed. "Pigeon stop play. He a West Indies Legend."

"Yes," said Lara, "we make pigeon fully fledged member of our club."

Riccardo and Crawfish spent the rest of the

afternoon entertaining the Legends with their songs.

This time the rain didn't let up and, at five o'clock, the umpires called the game off. West Indies and their pigeon had held out for a draw.

# Chapter 10

Early next morning Riccardo and Crawfish arrived at the airport for the flight home. Riccardo's head buzzed with his memories of London: he saw himself on stage at the Festival Hall; dancing with Christiane; in the rain at Lord's with Brian Lara, Sir Viv and all the other Legends and, of course, that pigeon. There were so many stories that he began to wonder how he would ever describe all his adventures to Bashy and his friends.

He blushed as he remembered cross-examining Brian Lara over Calypso's latest victory in Trinidad. They had beaten the Trinidad and Tobago junior champions by three wickets, thanks to an unbeaten score of 65 by Bashy.

"I not seen a finer innings from a young batter on a turning pitch in many a year," Lara had told him. When Bashy went in to bat, the bowlers had been well on top, but he'd taken the game away from them. He ended the proceedings with a six over long-on off the opening quick bowler. "If he keep progressing, one day we see him up there with the Legends," said Lara. "Heaven know West Indies need a young talent like that."

But as Riccardo waited in the check-in queue with Crawfish, these pleasant day dreams gave way to a more troubling thought. What was he going to tell his mother when he got home?

Talking about the Trinidad tournament Riccardo had found himself laughing and joking with his dad, just like the old days. He told him about the cricket matches he'd played: the dropped catches and fumbling fielding that had earned the name *Butter-Finger*, but also that miracle catch he'd pulled off, to his team mates' amazement, in the game that took Calypso through to the Trinidad tournament. And as he talked he forgot to be angry. He spoke to Nanny too and, as ever, she was friendly and kind – it was hard to dislike her.

Crawfish interrupted Riccardo's thoughts.

"If we arrive Port of Spain on time, you want go see the game?" he asked.

"What? The final?"

"Yes, Brian tell me they play only a mile or two from the airport. We can be there by tea time and catch the end of proceedings."

At the thought of seeing all his friends Riccardo momentarily forgot about his troubles... but then he was staring them in the face again. Walking across the busy departure terminal, were none other than his father and Nanny. Whatever were they doing here? Then he noticed that Nanny was carrying a baby in a sling over her shoulders.

"Say hello to your little sister, Keandra," she said, rushing up with a beaming smile.

"We decide you not want to leave London without meeting her," said his dad. Keandra gurgled and smiled happily.

"She have a fine singing voice just like her brother," said Crawfish.

"And she look like you, too," said Nanny. "Like two peas in the same pod... one little pea, one big."

"Maybe you write a song for she, Butter-Finger?" said Riccardo's father.

Keandra purred and grinned again. Riccardo couldn't take his eyes off her. Half an hour passed in a flash as he studied all his little sister's features and expressions. When finally he and Crawfish dashed off to the departure lounge, with only minutes to spare to catch their flight, Nanny gave him a kiss and his father hugged him. Riccardo noticed a tear running down his dad's cheek.

"See you again soon, son," he said. "I promise it not be too long this time."

The plane landed on time at Piarco International Airport. A few miles away Calypso Cricket Club was already in deep trouble. After the unexpected victories of the past week they were now facing a reality check. Their injuries weren't helping matters, either. Natty was only bowling at half pace and Bashy, unable to keep wicket with his broken finger, was fielding in the deep. Some of the other players were also looking tired and jaded.

Put in to bat by Alligator Pond on a bouncy pitch, they had been bowled out for just 76, crumbling against the Alligators' pace attack.

The Jamaican opening batters got off to a flier and were on 45 before the first wicket fell. After that, Calypso's bowlers fought hard to get back into the game and bagged three more wickets. But at 66 for 4 the match was slipping away from them fast. Was this the end of the road?

Then Leo took a hat-trick.

It was just as the third ball slammed into the stumps that Riccardo and Crawfish got out of their taxi. The crowd was in a huge state of excitement, screaming for Leo and Calypso. The underdogs had become the firm favourites of the locals who were dancing wildly to the rhythm of the now famous Calypso band. Wesley, the band's leader, was already singing a lively improvised celebration of Leo's amazing hat-trick.

Bashy was the first to spot Riccardo and he waved urgently to his friend. A glance at the scoreboard and Riccardo knew in a flash what Bashy wanted. It was time for a Butter-Finger song to rouse the players.

The band was set up in front of the pavilion and Wesley grinned broadly when he saw Riccardo approaching. He extended his fist and Riccardo gave it a soft punch. As Leo loped back to his mark,

Riccardo was at the mike to sing a burst of the song he'd started writing on the plane.

In the world of cricket, wonders never cease –
Now Alligator pad up at the crease.
People tell me if I seeing right
But I see Alligator in flannel white,
Facing a leather ball in full flight.

The words brought a smile to the faces around the ground. But Leo's grim expression didn't change. The fast bowler's eyes would have brought fear to the heart of any batter. Perhaps this was what *Whispering Death* looked like when he ran in, thought Riccardo... except there was no *whispering* about Leo. With his big shoulders and his sticking-out ears, it was little wonder everyone called him *Big Lug*.

Leo growled as he released the ball and it whistled past the edge of the bat, over the middle stump and into Ravi's gloves.

Riccardo sang again and the band played louder. The Trinie crowd knew all about Butter-Finger, but they'd never heard him 'live' before and they cheered at the end of every line of the song.

Yes, Butter-Finger live to see the day
Alligator play cricket the reptile way.
And it ain't fair, no it ain't fair,
Alligator ain't using bat or feet,
He defending the wicket with he teeth.


With the last ball of the over, Leo produced a straight yorker; it hammered into the batter's boot and up went the umpire's finger.

The game had been turned on its head in the space of one over. At 66 for eight, the Alligators were reeling. Bashy was Natty's surprise choice to bowl at the other end from Leo, yet he kept up the pressure with his crafty off-breaks. He only gave away two runs but Alligator Pond were creeping ever closer to their target.

Leo came back and the look in his eyes was scarier than ever. He was bowling like the wind and it was clear that something had to give. This time it went the Alligators' way – an edge flew over the slips to the vacant third-man boundary. Five to win and two wickets left. Suddenly the Jamaicans were sniffing victory again.

"Beat the ball, man!" shouted one.

"The boy chuckin'!" screamed another.

Riccardo sang louder still.

Alligator don't play fair – don't play fair,
Alligator make the umpire too scared
To put the finger of fate in the air –
Umpire dare not doubt Alligator stroke,
So umpire finger deep inside he coat.

A leg bye and an edged single took the score to 74 with the Alligators cheering every run.

Leo pounded in once more. It was the final ball of his allotted spell; everyone in ground knew it and most of them were urging Leo on for a final wicket. His shirt was tugging and tearing the wind as he reached the umpire.

Arching his back he seemed to rise to twice his natural height as his bowling arm came over in a blur. In the blink of an eye a perfect yorker ripped middle stump out of the turf. The batter later swore he'd never seen it. For a moment he stood open-mouthed, staring down at the wreckage of his wicket. Then he shook his head and walked off.

"That was fast, man," gasped Ravi, who was keeping wicket. He embraced Leo who had followed through the full length of the pitch.

"Lucky it strike the stumps, Ravi man. Else it go straight through you," said Leo, who could never be accused of modesty.

Riccardo sang:

Alligator don't play fair – don't play fair,
Alligator make the umpire too scared
To put the finger of fate in the air –
Umpire dare not doubt Alligator stroke,
So umpire finger deep inside he coat.

And when Alligator lose he middle stump
The umpire throat develop a lump.
Yes, my friend, every word I say is true,
The umpire shedding crocodile tears, too.
Lord, umpire shedding crocodile tears, too.

"Your turn now, Bash," said Natty calmy. "Finish them off."

Bashy's first ball was squirted into a gap and the Alligators ran a single. 75 for nine. Their team-mates cheered as if the batter had scored a hundred.

The band burst into action again and Riccardo tried his best to inspire his friend to grab the final wicket.

In the world of cricket, wonders never cease –
Now Alligator pad up at the crease.
People tell me if I seeing right
But I see Alligator in flannel white,
Facing a leather ball in full flight.

Bashy took the ball. The Alligators needed one to draw level, two to win. He calmly waited for the number 11 to settle at the wicket. Then he slowly and deliberately adjusted his field, building up the pressure on the batter. Leo came in from the boundary to a catching position. So did Cuthbert. There wasn't a sound around the ground except the rustle of the palm leaves.

The fielders walked in briskly as Bashy bowled. The ball squirmed off bat and pad towards the empty gully area and the batter raced down the pitch for the single that would have brought the scores level. But there was a loud scream of "No!" from the other end.

Turning and trying to scramble back to the

crease, the batter looked in horror as Natty, completely forgetting about his bad leg, stormed in from cover point. He picked up and threw in one movement and Ravi took the ball cleanly over the stumps and flicked off the bails.

# Chapter 11

The celebrations that followed the fall of Alligator Pond's last wicket reminded Riccardo of Henderson's words in London: "They don't celebrate too much in this country," he'd said. "We show them how to celebrate proper, eh?"

And this was going to be a proper Caribbean party... the band would make sure of that. Wesley and Riccardo saluted the victors, one by one, as they danced off the field. And long before Leo received his award they were acclaiming him in song as *Man-of-the-match Leo*.

The band stopped playing just long enough for Natty to limp up and receive the big silver trophy, grinning like a Cheshire Cat. As Valentine Shield champions, little Calypso had just become the most famous junior cricket team in the entire West Indies.

Leo was voted *man of the series* as well as *man of the match* and he made a short speech which no one could hear because he wasn't talking into the microphone. When the food arrived,

Riccardo and the band at last got a break from playing. 'The feast come courtesy of Mr Brian Lara,' announced a voice over the loudspeaker. There was so much of it that it was impossible to choose what to eat.

Riccardo found himself with a plateful of chilli prawns and goat curry and spice chicken. It was actually his second plateful, because he'd dropped the first one coming down the steps of the pavilion.

With all the singing and celebrating, Riccardo hadn't yet had a chance to speak to Bashy. He found him at last, talking to Count Crawfish.

"Hey, big city Butter-Finger!" said Bashy. "Count tell me you the star of London Town."

"And he tell you we meet Brian Lara at Lord's?" asked Riccardo.

"Wow, man!"

"And Michael Holding and Courtney Walsh and Sir Viv and ..."

"You dreaming, Riccardo?" said Bashy, looking to the Count to tell him that his friend was only joking.

"... and Clive Lloyd and Garry Sobers and ..." said Crawfish.

"Wow," said Bashy again and again.

Crawfish wandered off, chuckling to himself, and Riccardo was compelled to take Bashy through every moment of their day at Lord's. As he told the story of the pigeon he almost had to pinch himself to believe that it had happened only yesterday.

Then it was Bashy's turn and he gave Riccardo a ball-by-ball account of the whole Valentine Shield tournament, most of which he'd heard already from Brian Lara.

They'd been talking for nearly an hour before Riccardo spoke about the concert and the events that followed his appearance at the Royal Festival Hall.

"You see your dad!" said Bashy, wide-eyed.

"He there in the crowd."

"What you say to him?"

"Nothing. I not see him again till next day. Then I too angry to talk."

"Don't blame you, man. He give you a long walk these three year."

"I going to meet him again," said Riccardo.

"You go back to London?"

"One day soon. Or maybe he come here." He told Bashy about Nanny and baby Keandra.

"What you tell your ma?" asked Bashy, getting straight to the point.

For the hundred and first time, Riccardo thought about arriving home and seeing his mother and his sister and Jessie. Suddenly he knew what he was going to say.

"I tell them I see Dad in London," he said. "And we got to talk about it."

"So you forgive him?" asked Bashy.

Riccardo looked at his friend but said nothing. He thought of his father and Nanny and little Keandra and the beginnings of a song came drifting into his head:

I can stare all I want at your photo
But photo can't hug me and watch me grow.

"You forgive him?" asked Bashy again.

"No... I not sure... maybe someday," said Riccardo hesitantly.

He knew he loved his daddy every bit as much as before and that his daddy loved him. That's what he'd tell his mother. He was sure she would understand when he explained everything.

He pictured himself sitting at the table with Jessie, his dog, begging for food as she always did, and his mum and sister, Martha, listening to his long story and nodding. And then his mum reaching across the table and, with a tear in her eye, putting her hand gently on top of his.

One day he would write a song to his father to tell him how he felt. And it might just start like this:

I can stare all I want at your photo
But photo can't hug me and watch me grow.
It ain't too late for me daddy to play he role...
Tell me rhymes and stories from days of old.